GH🅾STBUSTERS™

PROUD TO BE A GHOSTBUSTER

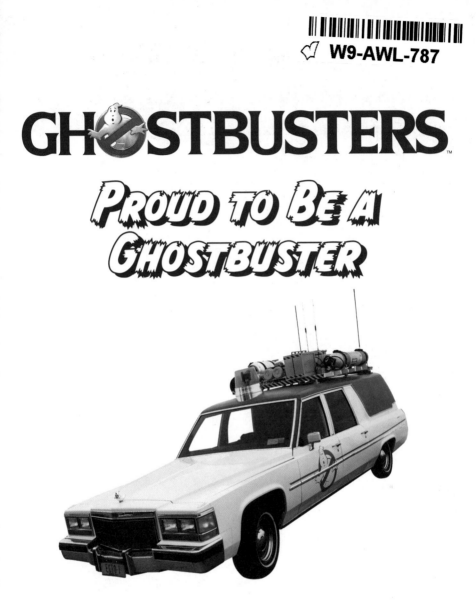

adapted by David Lewman

Ready-to-Read

Simon Spotlight

New York   London   Toronto   Sydney   New Delhi

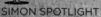

SIMON SPOTLIGHT
An imprint of Simon & Schuster Children's Publishing Division
1230 Avenue of the Americas, New York, New York 10020
This Simon Spotlight edition June 2016
Ghostbusters TM & © 2016 Columbia Pictures Industries, Inc. All rights reserved.
All rights reserved, including the right of reproduction in whole or in part in any form.
SIMON SPOTLIGHT, READY-TO-READ, and colophon are registered trademarks
of Simon & Schuster, Inc.
For information about special discounts for bulk purchases, please contact
Simon & Schuster Special Sales at 1-866-506-1949 or business@simonandschuster.com.
Designed by Brittany Naundorff
Manufactured in the United States of America 0516 LAK
10 9 8 7 6 5 4 3 2
ISBN 978-1-4814-7504-4 (hc)
ISBN 978-1-4814-7503-7 (pbk)
ISBN 978-1-4814-7505-1 (eBook)

CONTENTS

Meet Abby Yates and Erin Gilbert. If it weren't for these friends, the world would be full of ghosts, and everything would be terrible. They are an important pair, but their friendship almost fell apart—twice!

This is the story of how two friends became friends, unfriended each other, then became friends again, made two new friends, and how those four friends became the Ghostbusters.

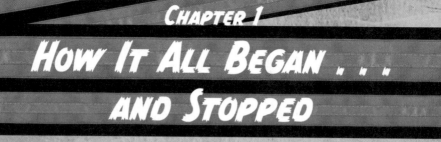

CHAPTER 1
HOW IT ALL BEGAN . . .
AND STOPPED

When Erin was eight years old, a terrifying ghost lady came into her room every night for a year! But after she told the kids at school, they made fun of her, calling her "ghost girl." Erin felt sad and alone.

Then Erin met Abby. She didn't call Erin "ghost girl." She *believed* Erin's story! They bonded right away. Thanks to Abby, Erin didn't feel alone anymore.

Together, they did a science fair project on the barrier that separated ghosts and people. Abby and Erin claimed that this barrier kept ghosts from coming into our world, but sometimes they broke through! When they were older, Abby and Erin wrote a book about ghosts.

Once their book came out, Erin got scared that people would tease her again for believing in ghosts. She was so nervous that she ditched her best friend.

Abby went on TV to defend the book on her own, and everyone made fun of her. It was Abby's turn to feel sad and alone.

After that, Erin and Abby didn't speak for a long time.

Abby didn't let Erin's fear stop her. She kept studying ghosts. After years of searching, one finally showed up at the Aldridge Mansion Museum in New York City. Erin also showed up that day and went on a ghost chase with Abby and Abby's new best friend, Jillian Holtzmann.

Once inside the museum, they pulled out their ghost detector and turned it on.

"Does that work?" Erin asked.

"Um, *yeah*, it works!" Abby said confidently. "We just haven't *seen* it work, because we haven't had direct contact with the paranormal. *Yet!*" Abby was clearly still mad at Erin.

11

As they walked around the museum, Abby's ghost detector lit up and started to spin! "I didn't even know it did that," Abby admitted.

A form started to take shape on a stairway. It was the ghost of a young woman. Her name had been Gertrude! Abby, Erin, and Holtzmann were amazed!

Abby said, "Careful!"

"Hello, ma'am," said Erin. "My name is—"

Gertrude opened her mouth wide and spewed slimy ectoplasm all over her! Yuck!

After Gertrude zoomed away, Erin asked, "What just happened?"

"I'll tell you what just happened," Abby said. "We saw a ghost!"

"We did!" Erin agreed. "We saw a ghost!"

Erin, Abby, and Holtzmann ran outside, celebrating. They jumped up and down and danced around!

"Ghosts are real! *Ghosts are real!*" they yelled.

It looked like Erin and Abby might be friends again. That was a *very* good thing because they were going to need each other.

Chapter 3
Ghostbusters Open for Business

Because of their ghosthunting, Abby, Erin, and Holtzmann were fired from their jobs. No one believed they had actually seen a ghost. They decided to move their gear into a Chinese restaurant and open a ghost-hunting business together. They even hired a receptionist, Kevin! Everyone contributed something to the team.

Holtzmann built all of the equipment they used to detect and trap ghosts. She made everything from PKE meters to proton blasters.

"She's a brilliant engineer," Abby told Erin.

"To be clear," Holtzmann said, "Nothing in this lab is safe."

Erin was excited to study ghosts again, and she wanted to do it the right way this time. She had been a physics professor at Columbia University and knew how to make discoveries by the book. Using scientific principles, she would show the world that ghosts were real!

Abby was their fearless leader. She was happy with her two best friends by her side and didn't care if anyone else believed them. The team was complete. All they needed was a ghost. Soon they would get their chance.

One day a stranger named Patty Tolan came to their door.

"I was just chased by a ghost," she said.

The Ghostbusters went to work! Patty showed them the spot in the subway where she'd seen the ghost . . . and the ghost reappeared!

"That is . . . unsettling," said Erin.
"Yeah, get some light on that,"
agreed Patty. They pointed their
flashlights on the skinny, creepy
ghost. They named him Sparky.

Holtzmann hooked up Erin to a proton box. "Don't move too much. Or talk. And definitely don't sweat," she told Erin. "Hey, look. He's getting closer."

Erin nervously fired the proton stream to hold Sparky in place.

Sparky was overpowering the proton stream! But that was the least of their problems.

Suddenly, a subway train appeared. The Ghostbusters picked up Erin and ran. They jumped out of the way just in time. The train went through Sparky and splattered them with ectoplasm! The Ghostbusters were slimed, but they were alive—thanks to their quick teamwork!

23

After, Patty asked to join the team. "I can borrow a car so you don't have to keep lugging that equipment," she said. She was also very smart. She knew a lot about New York City history.

"Welcome to the team!" said Abby. Now the group was truly complete.

CHAPTER 4
IT'S TOUGH BEING A GHOSTBUSTER

Everything was great inside the Ghostbusters' headquarters. Outside, though, the Ghostbusters were the laughing stock of the city. No one believed that ghosts were even real.

The teasing reminded Erin of when she was called "ghost girl." She was embarrassed to be a Ghostbuster. She wanted to catch a ghost so people would take her seriously again.

Thankfully, a ghost appeared at a rock concert. The Ghostbusters put on their jumpsuits and zoomed to the theater.

"Are you the Ghostbusters?" the manager asked. "You're dressed like garbage men!"

That was just the kind of teasing that embarrassed Erin.

Inside the concert hall, a ghost whirled above the crowd. The people in the audience thought the ghost was part of the rock band's act. They cheered.

Erin knew this was her chance to catch a ghost and prove they were real. "We can't let that ghost get away!" Erin yelled.

"All right, ladies! Light it up!" Abby shouted. The Ghostbusters aimed their proton blasters at the ghost. *ZAP!*

The Ghostbusters pulled the ghost into a trap. Holtzmann slammed the lid closed.

"Well," Erin said, "did we catch a ghost or not?"

"Oh," Holtzmann replied, "we caught a ghost."

"Yes!" Erin shouted.

"We did it!" Abby yelled.

The friends felt like they were on top of the world. They pretended to play their proton blasters like guitars, and the crowd went wild!

But when the Ghostbusters got back to headquarters, they discovered they were still being teased. Erin decided she would prove they had trapped a ghost. She walked up to the trap and pressed a button to open the lid . . . and the ghost escaped and flew out the window!

That was the last straw. "We look like maniacs," Erin complained to Abby. "I know you don't care, but I do."

"I've been called 'weird,'" Abby said, "but I focus on what matters. We discover all sorts of new things. I get to work with my friends. I feel lucky."

Erin didn't feel lucky, though. She wanted to be taken seriously. For the second time, the friends parted ways.

The Ghostbusters didn't know it yet, but they were going to need Erin for their biggest case ever.

CHAPTER 5

THEIR BIGGEST CASE EVER

Gertrude, Sparky, and all the other ghosts appearing in the city were part of a big evil plan. A bad guy named Rowan was opening the barrier to the ghost world. If he succeeded, there would be ghosts everywhere!

Erin was at home when she figured out Rowan's plan. She had to warn the Ghostbusters! She called their headquarters, but no one answered the phone. She took off on her own.

Meanwhile, evil Rowan had become a ghost. He had taken control over poor Kevin! The Ghostbusters had to save Kevin.

Abby called Erin for help, but she wasn't at home. "She's never there when you need her," Abby said angrily.

They jumped into Ecto-1, their car, and followed Rowan and Kevin. Rowan started letting ghost after ghost through an opening in the barrier. The ghosts were pouring through the portal into New York City! There was no way they could stop him without Erin's help. It was a job for the whole Ghostbusters team.

Just then Erin found her friends. "Couldn't let you have all the fun," Erin joked.

Everyone was glad to see her. Together, the Ghostbusters freed Kevin from Rowan and sent all the ghosts back to their world.

Only Rowan remained. "He's too strong," Erin said. "We can't let the portal close with him still here!"

Then Abby got a crazy idea.

CHAPTER 6
GHOSTBUSTERS . . .
AND PROUD OF IT!

"Hey!" Abby yelled at Rowan, zapping him with her proton stream. He growled at her. "I have his attention," she said and ran toward the portal. Rowan chased her all the way through it.

"Abby!" Erin cried as her friend disappeared. Erin grabbed a cable and jumped through the portal after her. She had to save Abby.

Patty and Holtzmann tried to keep the portal open, but it was closing forever.

Suddenly, Abby and Erin came flying back out on the cable. Their hair was white from being on the "other side." The portal closed and all the ghosts were gone.

"We did it?" Abby asked, stunned.

"We all did it," said Erin, thankful for her fellow "ghost girls."

"That's right," said Kevin, appearing out of nowhere. "We all did it."

"What did you do?" asked Erin.

"I went over to that power box, pushed a few buttons, and then everything got sucked into the portal, and it closed up," said Kevin.

"That had nothing to do with anything—" Erin said to Kevin, but Abby interrupted.

"No, that may have helped," Abby lied. "Good for you, Kevin!"

"Anyway, let's not turn on each other now," said Kevin. "That's not what Ghostbusters are about." Nobody could argue with that.

Erin and Abby mended their friendship for good that day. According to Holtzmann, though, the Ghostbusters weren't just friends. They were family.